Dear Parent:
Your child's love of reading starts here!

Every child learns to read in a different way and at his or her own speed. Some go back and forth between reading levels and read favorite books again and again. Others read through each level in order. You can help your young reader improve and become more confident by encouraging his or her own interests and abilities. From books your child reads with you to the first books he or she reads alone, there are I Can Read Books for every stage of reading:

SHARED READING
Basic language, word repetition, and whimsical illustrations, ideal for sharing with your emergent reader

BEGINNING READING
Short sentences, familiar words, and simple concepts for children eager to read on their own

READING WITH HELP
Engaging stories, longer sentences, and language play for developing readers

READING ALONE
Complex plots, challenging vocabulary, and high-interest topics for the independent reader

ADVANCED READING
Short paragraphs, chapters, and exciting themes for the perfect bridge to chapter books

I Can Read Books have introduced children to the joy of reading since 1957. Featuring award-winning authors and illustrators and a fabulous cast of beloved characters, I Can Read Books set the standard for beginning readers.

A lifetime of discovery begins with the magical words "I Can Read!"

Visit www.icanread.com for information
on enriching your child's reading experience.

For Lisa and Allan,
one really neat couple!
—H. P.

For Linda and Liz—
you always have good stuff!
—L. A.

Gouache and black pencil were used to prepare the full-color art.

I Can Read Book® is a trademark of HarperCollins Publishers.

Amelia Bedelia is a registered trademark of Peppermint Partners, LLC.

Library of Congress Cataloging-in-Publication Data

Parish, Herman.

Amelia Bedelia by the yard / by Herman Parish ; pictures by Lynne Avril.

  pages cm.—(I can read. Level 1)

"Greenwillow Books."

Summary: "Amelia Bedelia's mother loves garage sales so much, she decides to have one herself! But Amelia Bedelia loves her garage and does not want to sell it, so she and her parents decide to call it a yard sale instead. People come from all over the neighborhood to buy Amelia Bedelia's family's old things, and one woman even buys the yard!"—Provided by publisher.

ISBN 978-0-06-233428-2 (hardback)—ISBN 978-0-06-233427-5 (pbk) [1. Mothers and daughters—Fiction. 2. Garage sales—Fiction. 3. Humorous stories.] I. Avril, Lynne, (date) illustrator. II. Title.

PZ7.P2185Aoa 2015 [E]—dc23 2015014190

19 20 LSCC 15 14 13 12 First Edition

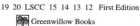
Greenwillow Books

I Can Read!

BEGINNING
1
READING

Amelia Bedelia
· By the Yard ·

by Herman Parish ✿ pictures by Lynne Avril

Greenwillow Books, *An Imprint of* HarperCollins*Publishers*

Amelia Bedelia and her parents
were coming home from the park.
They drove by a sign.
Amelia Bedelia's mother shouted,
"Pull over, pull over!"

Amelia Bedelia looked out her window.

She did not see a pullover sweater.

She did see lots of stuff for sale.

All the stuff was spread out

in someone's front yard.

Amelia Bedelia's mother

jumped out of the car.

"Mom loves garage sales,"
said Amelia Bedelia's father.
"Is she buying a new garage?"
asked Amelia Bedelia.

Amelia Bedelia's father shook his head.

"No, but we could use another garage

just to hold all the stuff she buys

at garage sales," he said.

Amelia Bedelia's mother
brought back two treasures.

She handed a book
to Amelia Bedelia.

She tossed a sweater
to Amelia Bedelia's father.
"It's a pullover," she said.

"Is that the one you saw
from the car?"
said Amelia Bedelia.

10

Amelia Bedelia's father had already
pulled the sweater over his head.

"Did you hear about the big garage sale
next Saturday?" he said.

"Where?" asked Amelia Bedelia's mother.

"At our house," he said.

"Let's get rid of our clutter.
We need to weed out!"

For the next week,

Amelia Bedelia and her parents

sorted through the things

they had not used in years.

By Saturday, they were ready

for their very own garage sale—

except for one thing.

Amelia Bedelia was not happy

about their sign.

"You can't sell our garage,"

said Amelia Bedelia.

"Where will our car sleep?

Plus, the garage matches our house."

"Oh, honey,"

said Amelia Bedelia's mother.

"We'd never sell our garage!"

"Let's try a different idea,"

said Amelia Bedelia's father.

He held up a new sign.

"Is this better?"

"No!" wailed Amelia Bedelia.
"That is worse. I love our yard
even more than our garage."

"Okay. We will not sell either one,"
said Amelia Bedelia's mother.
"We will just sell the things
we put in the yard."

People began stopping to look.

It got crowded fast.

Amelia Bedelia's

parents were busy.

Amelia Bedelia helped, too.

"Nice sewing machine," said a woman.

"Can you throw in a yardstick?"

"Sure,"
said Amelia Bedelia.
She ran behind the garage.

There was a big pile
of leaves and sticks there.
She got as many sticks
as she could carry.

"Here you go,"
said Amelia Bedelia.
"These sticks are
from our yard.
Pick one.
I'll throw it in."

21

The lady laughed.

"I am looking for a yardstick

that is thirty-six inches long," she said.

Amelia Bedelia grabbed a tall ruler

from a messy box of stuff.

She used it to measure the longest stick.

"This one is exactly

thirty-six inches!" she said.

"Perfect," said the woman.

"If I buy the sewing machine,

will you throw in that ruler, too?"

"I will hand it to you," said Amelia Bedelia.

"It's a deal," said the woman.

She looked around the yard.

"I am making curtains," she said.

"I will need yards of fabric."

"Yards?" said Amelia Bedelia.
"That is a lot of fabric.
That would cover up
my mom's flowers."

"The flowers are beautiful," said the woman.

"I would love to buy some of her plants."

"You can," said Amelia Bedelia.

"My dad says we are weeding out.

Everything in the yard is for sale."

Amelia Bedelia found a shovel.

She dug up some plants for the woman.

By the end of the day, everything was sold.

Amelia Bedelia's parents

were shocked to see the holes in their yard.

"Amazing," said Amelia Bedelia's father.

"At our yard sale, even the yard got sold."

Amelia Bedelia's mother sighed.

"Who would buy the yard?" she asked.

"A nice lady," said Amelia Bedelia.

"She does everything by the yard."

"Well," said Amelia Bedelia's mother.

"My plants will grow back soon.

I do like getting rid of clutter.

It makes things easier to find."

"The only thing I want to find

is a pizza," said Amelia Bedelia's father.

31

On the way to the pizza place,

they passed another sign.

And this time, Amelia Bedelia's mother

did not say a single word.